POLLY PAINT
- WHAT DO YOU DO? -

Written by
Gemma Merlen

Illustrated by
Adele Booth

To Harriet
Enjoy!
Gemma M

I would like to thank my family and friends for their unswerving support.

Thank you Jane, Sam, Thomas, Joseph, Erika and April for reading the story first and giving me the confidence to show it to everyone else.

Thank you Becky Bowyer for your skilled editing and insights.

Huge thank you to Adele Booth for bringing these characters to life so beautifully.

And finally thank you to my little herd for many years of happiness, pride and perpetual exposure to the Great British weather.

Polly Paint was nearly two
when Mother Mare said, 'Look at you!

'My lovely foal you're growing tall,
you're ready for the big wide world.

'You must now go to your new home,
it has space to grow and learn and roam.

'Be kind and gentle, that's my advice.
'Be curious, be humorous and always be nice.

Good luck, my daughter, be good not bad.
Your life awaits you, be happy not sad.'

Polly Paint was shocked and scared,
that she should leave her Mother Mare.

She thought she knew the whole wide world.
Surely that was her stable, barn and field?

Polly Paint wanted to feel brave
but she unsure of how she should behave.

She tossed her head and snorted loud,
'I will make my mother proud.

'I am young, I am fun, I will dazzle everyone.
'I'm pretty, I'm witty all can see,
so everyone will make friends with me.'

Off she went to somewhere new.
Green fields, tall trees tickled skies of blue.

She looked around her and sure enough,
she spied some ponies and trotted off.

'I'm Polly Paint,' she called out loud.
'I'm young, I'm fun, I'm ever so proud,

With a beautiful coat and shiny hooves.
Come and catch my fancy moves.'

Not one pony looked her way.
Polly Paint felt dismay.

She drew a breath and swished her tail,
she'd never known any kind of fail.

Polly Paint found a tiny pony and twirled around.
The smallest pony stood her ground.

'I'm Polly Paint,' the youngster called.
'Look, my coat is bay skewbald.

'I am young, I am fun, I will dazzle everyone.
'I'm pretty, I'm witty all can see.
'Do you want to be friends with me?'

'I'm Little Lily,' the pony said.
She blinked her eyes and dropped her head.

Polly Paint was confused.
She tossed her mane and stamped her hooves.

'Don't you want to come and play?
It's more fun than staying here all day!'

Little Lily answered in her squeaky way, 'I will not leave, I want to stay.
'My family here keep me safe and I have found my special place.

'I am the smallest as you see, it matters not my size is wee,
'My herd are always by my side, so nothing scary makes me hide.
'Maybe you can join us too, but if you did what would you do?'

Polly Paint trotted to a golden pony where she grazed.
The golden pony munched unfazed.

'I'm Polly Paint,' the youngster called.
'Look, my coat is bay skewbald,

'I am young, I am fun, I will dazzle everyone,
'I'm pretty, I'm witty all can see,
'Do you want to be friends with me?'

'I'm Sunshine Sally,' the pony said.
She twitched her ears and shook her head.

Polly Paint was confused.
She tossed her mane and stamped her hooves.

'Don't you want to come and play?
'It's more fun than grazing here all day!'

Sunshine Sally answered in her gentle way,
'I'll not leave, I want to stay.

'My family here keep me safe and
I have found my special place.

'I'm the slowest pony, I'm always last,
but it doesn't matter I'm not fast,

'My heart is big, I'm very kind
and I am placid all the time.

'Maybe you can join us too,
but if you did what would you do?'

Polly Paint met a fluffy pony way up the field.
The fluffy pony didn't yield.

'I'm Polly Paint,' the youngster called.
'Look, my coat is bay skewbald,

'I am young, I am fun, I will dazzle everyone.
'I'm pretty, I'm witty all can see.
'Do you want to be friends with me?'

'I'm Speedy Marmot,' the pony said.
He pawed the ground and flicked his head.

Polly Paint was confused.
She tossed her mane and stamped her hooves.

'Don't you want to come and play?
'It's more fun than staying here all day!'

Speedy Marmot answered in his chirpy way,
'I'll not leave, I want to stay.

'My family here keep me safe
and I have found my special place.

'I'm the fastest pony, I love to run,
so I keep watch on everyone.

'When I race I'm just a blur,
of mane and legs and dark brown fur.

'Maybe you can join us too,
but if you did what would you do?'

Polly Paint found an old pony
in the shade of a tree.

The oldest pony didn't flee.
'I'm Polly Paint,' the youngster called.
'Look, my coat is bay skewbald.

'I am young, I am fun, I will dazzle everyone.
'I'm pretty, I'm witty all can see.
'Do you want to be friends with me?'

'I'm Freckled Fonz,' the pony said.
He swished his tail and rubbed his head.

Polly Paint was confused.
She tossed her mane and stamped her hooves.

'Don't you want to come and play?
It's more fun than resting here all day!'

Freckled Fonz answered in his mellow way,
'I will not leave, I want to stay.

'My family here keep me safe
and I have found my special place.

'I'm the oldest pony, I can no longer see,
I trust my herd to take care of me.

'I tell stories that make them smile,
about my younger years when I was wild!

'Maybe you can join us too,
but if you did what would you do?'

Polly Paint finally found the biggest mare,
who waited patiently for her to share.

'I'm Polly Paint,' the youngster called.
'Look, my coat is bay skewbald.

'I am young, I am fun, I will dazzle everyone.
'I'm pretty, I'm witty all can see.
'Do you want to be friends with me?'

Polly Paint was confused.
She tossed her mane and stamped her hooves.

'Don't you want to come and play?
'It's more fun than standing here all day!'

'I'm Champion Chica,' the big horse said.
She kicked the ground and flung her head.

Champion Chica answered in her charming way,
'I will not leave, I want to stay.

'I've had adventures and I am smart,
'I lead this herd, this is my part.

'I know my group, we are a team.
'We get along just like a dream.

'We each fill a unique space –
'We all deserve our special place.'

Polly realised this mare was beautiful and wise.
But there was kindness in her eyes.

Polly Paint turned and ran, to be alone.
She suddenly felt very far from home.

She missed Mother Mare and the paddock green,
where she pranced and danced just like a queen.

Poor Polly had to think what to say,
to persuade the herd to let her stay.

Searching her heart, she lifted her chin,
it was she knew, the time to begin.

Slowly she walked, with head down low,
and joined the five ponies stood in a row.

'Polly Paint you are bonny, you are tall,
but that's not enough to join us all.

'What would you do if we let you be,
the newest member of our family?'

Polly Paint looked at the ground.
She worried the others might still frown.

'I am light of foot and I can prance.
I love to spin and jump and dance.

'I want to join your family,
so I learn to be the best of me.

'Chica, please teach me grace and poise.
'Fonz, please help me know my voice.

'Sally, please teach me to stay calm
and Lily, please show me round the farm.

'I'd love to race Marmot up the hill,
but I'm sure he would be the fastest still.'

There was a moment when all were hushed.
Then Fonz shouted, 'Hooray! She's one of us!'

Chica snorted and kicked up her heels.
Sally and Lily let out squeals.

'Welcome Polly!' Marmot yelled and sped off in a furry blur.
Chica gently blew on Polly's face

And Polly knew she'd found her special place.

Did you see a little cat sitting on the ground?
We'd love to know her story too, but she's nowhere to be found!

She strolls around the field when the sun is overhead.
But if it's cold or wet outside she curls up snug in bed.